A Connecticut Yankee in King Arthur's Court

Mark Twain

ILLUSTRATED

Pendulum Press, Inc.

West Haven, Connecticut

ISBN 0-88301-093-3 Complete Set
       0-88301-263-4 This Volume

Library of Congress Catalog Card Number 77-79436

Published by
Pendulum Press, Inc.
An Academic Industries, Inc. Company
The Academic Building
Saw Mill Road
West Haven, Connecticut 06516

Printed in the United States of America

to the teacher

Pendulum Press is proud to offer the NOW AGE ILLUSTRATED Series to schools throughout the country. This completely new series has been prepared by the finest artists and illustrators from around the world. The script adaptations have been prepared by professional writers and revised by qualified reading consultants.

Implicit in the development of the Series are several assumptions. Within the limits of propriety, anything a child reads and/or wants to read is *per se* an educational tool. Educators have long recognized this and have clamored for materials that incorporate this premise. The sustained popularity of the illustrated format, for example, has been documented, but it has not been fully utilized for educational purposes. Out of this realization, the NOW AGE ILLUSTRATED Series evolved.

In the actual reading process, the illustrated panel encourages and supports the student's desire to read printed words. The combination of words and picture helps the student to a greater understanding of the subject; and understanding, that comes from reading, creates the desire for more reading.

The final assumption is that reading as an end in itself is self-defeating. Children are motivated to read material that satisfies their quest for knowledge and understanding of their world. In this series, they are exposed to some of the greatest stories, authors, and characters in the English language. The Series will stimulate their desire to read the original edition when their reading skills are sufficiently developed. More importantly, reading books in the NOW AGE ILLUSTRATED Series will help students establish a mental "pegboard" of information—images, names, and concepts—to which they are exposed. Let's assume, for example, that a child sees a television commercial which features Huck Finn in some way. If he has read the NOW AGE Huck Finn, the TV reference has meaning for him which gives the child a surge of satisfaction and accomplishment.

After using the NOW AGE ILLUSTRATED editions, we know that you will share our enthusiasm about the series and its concept.

—The Editors

about the author

Samuel Langhorne Clemens was born in 1835 in Florida, Missouri. Later he and his family moved to Hannibal, Missouri. Since Hannibal was on the Mississippi River, one of Clemens' earliest ambitions was to be a cub pilot on a riverboat.

Mark Twain, the pen-name Clemens adopted, means two fathoms or safe water. Undoubtedly, he chose the name because of his love for life on the river, which is revealed in *Huckleberry Finn*. This novel becomes an embodiment of the dreams of American boyhood.

Twain had a gift for combining the humorous with the serious. His characters are real and believable. In *A Connecticut Yankee in King Arthur's Court,* even Merlin the magician and Queen Morgan Le Fay act like ordinary people. They reveal the same anger, fear, and jealousy that all of us feel.

Throughout his life, Twain was always busy learning new things. Besides a writer of many successful novels, he was also a printer, riverboat pilot, journalist, travel writer, and publisher at one time or another. It is this wide range of experience, perhaps, that gives such flavor and vitality to his works. This great American author died at the age of seventy-five in Redding, Connecticut.

Samuel Clemens

A Connecticut Yankee In King Arthur's Court

Adapted by
JOHN NORWOOD FAGO

Illustrated by
FRANCISCO REDONDO

a
VINCENT FAGO
production

Sandy

Clarence

Hank Morgan
"A Connecticut Yankee"

King Arthur

Merlin the Magician

It was in Warwick Castle, an old building in England, that I, Mark Twain, met the stranger whose story you are about to read. We were at the very edge of a group taking a tour of the castle when he began speaking to me.

He turned to me and said something strange. He spoke as simply about this as someone else might have talked about the weather.

Do you believe that people can move backwards through time? Do you believe, for instance, that I myself could have been at King Arthur's Round Table?

As he talked, he seemed to drift in and out of this world and time. He spoke as though he had known Sir Lancelot, Sir Galahad, and all the other great men of King Arthur's court. *

*a king and his knights who lived in England during the sixth century

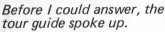

Before I could answer, the tour guide spoke up.

See the small hole through this armor? It must have been made after guns were invented.

My friend smiled a strange smile.

Believe it or not, I saw it happen!

By the time I got over my surprise at what he had said, he was gone. But later that night he came to see me.

LAUNCELOT

I made him welcome and gave him a hot drink, hoping he would tell his story. He soon began.

I am a Yankee* from Connecticut and a very handy man. My father was a blacksmith and my uncle was a horse doctor. I started work as both.

*a person who lives in any one of the six New England states

But I learned my real trade in a gun factory. I learned to make everything: guns, boilers, engines, anything at all. So they made me the boss.

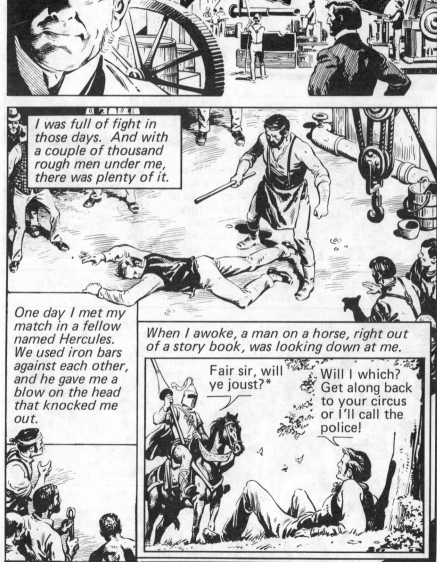

I was full of fight in those days. And with a couple of thousand rough men under me, there was plenty of it.

One day I met my match in a fellow named Hercules. We used iron bars against each other, and he gave me a blow on the head that knocked me out.

When I awoke, a man on a horse, right out of a story book, was looking down at me.

Fair sir, will ye joust?*

Will I which? Get along back to your circus or I'll call the police!

*a fight on horseback between two knights

He took me prisoner!

Is that Bridgeport, Connecticut?

No, Camelot, England.

The stranger grew too sleepy to continue. But he said he had written the story down and would let me read it.

After taking him to his room and helping him to bed, I returned to my own room with the story. I began reading as follows:

KING ARTHUR'S COURT
HANK MORGAN

The knight took me to a castle where we entered a huge paved court. I spoke to a young lad standing near me.

Where am I? What year is it? And who are you?

This is King Arthur's court. It is June 20th in the year 528. And I am Clarence.

My heart sank. I had left Connecticut in 1879. I was now thirteen hundred years in the past!

It was hard to believe, but I remembered that on June 21, 528, a total eclipse* of the sun had taken place.

If I am really back in King Arthur's time, I will be able to tell the future!

As for the Round Table, it looked like a circus to me. The knights were taking turns bragging to the king about all the great things they had done.

Then it was time for Sir Kay to tell his story. He was the knight who had brought me here.

What lies he told! He claimed that he had seen me kill thirteen brave knights before he had captured me.

*a blocking out of the sun's light; this happens when the moon passes between the sun and the earth

Before I could speak, the king sentenced me to die at noon on June 21st. My clothes were taken from me.

The next moment I found myself in the dungeon* with moldy straw for a bed and some rats for company. But I fell asleep in spite of it all.

Am I still dreaming?

It's no dream that you're to be burned at the stake!

Worse still, Merlin, the king's magician,** hath cast a spell on any who would help you. If you tell anyone, I'll be lost!

Merlin! Why, that crazy old man with his silly beliefs!

But it suddenly came to me that if everyone here was so afraid of Merlin's magic, perhaps I could work out a plan.

*an underground prison
**someone who performs magic tricks

The plan had worked. By the time they got me untied, the eclipse was total.

Let the magic pass away!

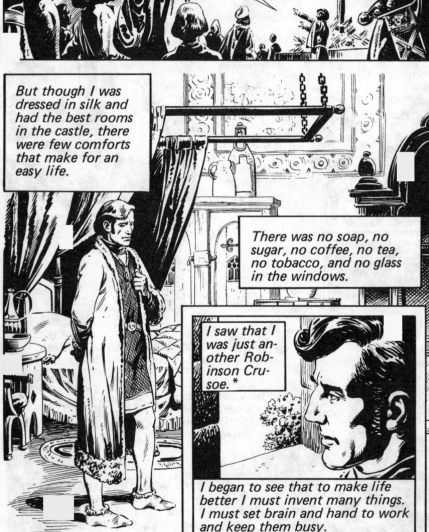

But though I was dressed in silk and had the best rooms in the castle, there were few comforts that make for an easy life.

There was no soap, no sugar, no coffee, no tea, no tobacco, and no glass in the windows.

I saw that I was just another Robinson Crusoe. *

I began to see that to make life better I must invent many things. I must set brain and hand to work and keep them busy.

*a man shipwrecked on a lonely island who managed to stay alive and well for many years

The eclipse had scared the people almost to death. Thousands came to see me perform another great deed.

This turned Merlin green with envy. He started a report that I was not a magician. I knew that something had to be done—and soon!

To give me time, I had Merlin thrown into prison. Then I told everyone that I would blow up Merlin's tower by fires from heaven.

I told Clarence that this was the kind of magic that had to be worked on first. We set about making a few bushels of blasting powder and a lightning rod.

Working by night, we laid the explosives. On the thirteenth night we placed the lightning rod. Then we waited until the next afternoon for the thunderstorm that was expected.

I had Merlin set free and sent over to meet me in front of the tower.

I am going to call down fire and blow up your tower. But first, I'll give you a chance to break my magic and stop the fire. Go ahead!

Do not worry. I can and I will!

He began to mutter and slowly worked himself into a trance. I waited until the coming storm reached us and then I faced him.

ALLA BOP! Magic stop!

It was a great bit of magic. A streak of lightning set off the blasting powder, and the tower blew up in a fountain of fire!

Your magic is weak. Now it is my turn!

The crowds left in a hurry. And for the time being, no one in the kingdom thought it wise to meddle in my affairs.

It was a strange country. Everyone seemed to live for only one reason: to crawl before the king, the Church, and the nobles.

I could have become a noble easily enough, but I didn't really want to be one. I suppose I just wasn't brought up that way!

But one day I did receive a fitting title. It fell from the lips of a blacksmith, and it stuck.

All hail! The Boss cometh!

It caught on and passed from mouth to mouth with a knowing smile. In ten days it was as familiar as the king's name.

They were always having grand tournaments* at Camelot. But to me they seemed like silly human bullfights.

One day I was the victim of one of those jokes where the teller does all the laughing and the listener just looks a little bit sick.

Sir Dinadan was about the worst joke-teller and the biggest bore. As he rode away after one of his long stories I said something I shouldn't have.

I hope he gets killed!

However, another knight, Sir Sagramor, heard my remark and thought I meant it for him. He became angry and wanted to fight.

But the fight was set for several years in the future. Sir Sagramor was about to leave in search of the Holy Grail** and this always took the knights a long time.

*fighting matches between the knights
**the cup used by Christ at the Last Supper

At the Round Table, the fight was much talked over. King Arthur thought I should set forth in search of great adventures so that I might become famous. Then I would also be more worthy to fight with Sir Sagramor.

But I talked my way out of it, saying that I had too many machines to oil up and keep running.

I had the beginning of all sorts of secret factories under way.

My schools, too, were doing well.

With the kingdom at my command, I had the nineteenth century booming right under the noses of these people from the Dark Ages.

But one day, after some years, a young girl came to King Arthur asking for help.

Although all the knights begged to be chosen, the king picked me, and I hadn't even asked.

Her friend and several others were being held in a castle. It was owned by three men who had one eye . . . or some such silly thing.

I left all my work in the hands of young Clarence and started off.

Soon I was swimming in rivers of sweat inside my iron suit. And the girl, Alisande le Carteloise, whom I called Sandy, was a blabbermouth. She could talk all week without stopping.

Take a rest, Sandy. The way you're using up air, we'll have to start bringing it in from somewhere else.

That night it rained. With the bugs and ants crawling around inside my armor, I swore I'd never wear it again.

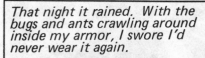

I hardly slept at all, but we left again at dawn. I walked behind, for I couldn't even reach the horse's back.

We came upon a group of poor workers. They were trying to mend the sorry thing that they called a road.

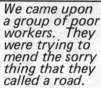

When I asked to eat with them, they couldn't believe I meant it. Sandy, for her part, said that she would rather eat with the cattle.

As we talked together, I asked them whether if every man had a free vote, they'd vote to have one family rule over them forever.

They seemed shocked by my question. But after a little thought, one of them seemed to understand what I was talking about.

He answered that it would be a crime to steal from a nation the will and choice of its people.

I took this man aside from the rest of this herd of human sheep.

Take this to Camelot and give it to Clarence. He will understand.

LET'S HELP THIS MAN TO FREE HIMSELF. PUT HIM INTO THE LEARNING FACTORIES.

I gave them three cents for my breakfast. In their money this was enough for a dozen breakfasts.

Then they helped Sandy and me back onto the horse, and I lit my pipe.

They thought that I had turned into a fire-breathing dragon. The only way I could get them to come back was to say that this was only part of my magic. It would harm no one but my enemies.

But I had learned something which quite soon was of great value!

Defend yourself, Lord! Here comes great danger!

Sandy got down, and I lit my pipe. I blew smoke through my helmet, and it stopped them dead in their tracks.

Very good! They wait for you.

Really? Is that true?

Sandy ran over and told them that I was The Boss. She said this "filled them with fear and dread". They agreed to go to King Arthur's court as my knights. She managed the thing better than I could have myself.

So we rode on with Sandy yapping away in my ear.

It did seem a pity that these strong men, who wasted so much time in battle, could not be given some useful work to do.

By and by we came to a castle.

To my relief, along came one of the knights working for me.

I was secretly hoping to make the knights look silly . . . and at the same time to teach them to be clean.

PERSIMMON'S SOAP

IT WORKS WONDERS

The sandwich sign* knight told us that the castle belonged to Morgan Le Fay, King Arthur's sister. She was known for her cruel and evil ways. Still, I wanted to meet her.

*a type of advertising sign made to be worn over a person's shoulders

Forgetting how she hated her brother, I said a kind word about King Arthur.

Take these people to the dungeons!

That struck cold on my ears, for her dungeons were known to be nasty places.

Morgan Le Fay, do you know what you are doing? This is *The Boss* you are dealing with!

I would never have thought of such a simple idea. But Morgan le Fay was frightened by my very name!

Er, yes. I just played this little jest hoping you'd show your art. Perhaps you could blast the guards to ashes with fire!

Just then we were called to dinner. Some musicians opened the feast with a song that sounded like a funeral hymn.

The queen was not pleased and had them all hanged after dinner.

Then the mighty feeding began. There was no talking, just rows of teeth opening and closing together, They sounded like the hum of a huge machine.

This went on for hours. Then at midnight . . .

The curse of God upon you, woman of no pity! You have killed my grandson without a just cause!

This scared everyone. To these people, a curse was an awful thing.

To everyone, that is, but Morgan Le Fay!

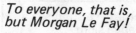

Burn her!

Sandy gave me a look and I knew she had another idea.

The Boss says this may not be! Stop at once or he will destroy your castle!

Le Fay gave in, and the crowd rushed to the door like a mob.

The queen had become so quiet that I called in another group of musicians to play for us. But they were worse than the others, so I didn't object when she decided to hang them too.

What was that?

Come. Ye shall see a strange sight!

We were about to go to bed when there came a faraway cry.

Some poor farmer was being tortured to confess shooting a deer. All of this was happening so that Morgan Le Fay could take his property after she had him killed.

Quick as a wink I put an end to it and cleared the room.

I'll send you both to my factory. You'll like it there.

My conscience* is more trouble to me than anything else I have. But in the morning I knew that I had to check the dungeons in this castle.

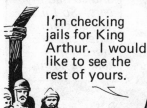

I'm checking jails for King Arthur. I would like to see the rest of yours.

She wasn't happy about it, but finally agreed to give us a tour.

The poor people I saw there had been shut away for very small crimes!

The newest prisoner had simply said it was his belief that without clothes you couldn't tell the king from a poor man. Here was someone with brains! I sent him to the factory also.

I freed them all.

*the part of our minds which helps us know right from wrong

She was surely a strange one, that Morgan Le Fay. I was glad to be on the road again.

Sandy's jaw had had a long rest and so had my ears. So I just stayed calm when she started in talking again.

Peradventure my head being distraught by the manifold matters whereunto . . .

Two days later, Sandy told me the castle was near.

The castle! Lo, there it is!

Castle? It's nothing but a pigsty!

No! It has been changed by magic!

Sandy began to cry, and I knew what I had to do. She saw the castle, I saw the pigsty. To argue with her would have been a waste of time.

I suppose this was a common case. Magic makes something appear strange to one person, but to another it has not changed at all.

Be careful, fair sir. There is fearful power here!

I bought all the hogs for sixteen cents and sent the grateful farmers away before calling Sandy. Then she had a happy talk with her long-lost princesses. To me they still looked like hogs.

Then we had to drive those awful hogs—that is, princesses—home, which was ten miles away.

Where is your family, Sandy?

I understand you not! I have no family!

Then whose house is this?

Why, I would tell you if I but knew myself!

But do you dream they would question the honor of such noble company?

It's an even bet that this is the first time they've had a treat like this!

Well, I had never seen anything like it! Sandy saw princesses and I could only see hogs! Anyway, she gave them a tearful farewell, and I turned the herd over to the servants.

*We came upon a group of happy, singing pilgrims. ***

They journey to the Valley of Holiness to drink the healing waters and to be blessed by the godly men who live there.

It was a famous spot where, by a miracle, waters had burst forth in a desert place. We decided to join the pilgrims so that I might learn more about life in the kingdom.

*people who travel to a holy place to receive a blessing

He was another one that I had put to some useful work. This fellow was in the hat line. That he also looked funny was part of my plan.

We stayed at an inn that night. In the morning I looked out and saw one of my knights riding up.

What news of the Valley of Holiness, friend?

The fountain has been dry for nine days! They sent for thee, *Sir Boss,* but found Merlin instead. He is there trying to work his magic this very moment!

I quickly made out a note and handed it to the knight.

Chemical department.
Send two of size #1
and two of size #3.
Also send two of my
trained men.
Sir Boss

Take this to Clarence in Camelot as fast as you can ride. Tell him to fill the order and send it to the Valley of Holiness quickly!

I will, *Sir Boss!*

Now that the thing they had come for had been ruined, the pilgrims were even more excited about seeing the place where it used to be.

Delay not, son! Get to thy work and start the water flowing again!

It will not do to mix our magic, Father. I can't touch the job until Merlin gives it up.

If Merlin had only used his eyes instead of his brain, he could have fixed the well himself.

But these simple people would have dried up and blown away without thinking of going down the well. There they could find out what was really the matter.

This is a job of magic that will strain my powers to the limit! But we will try if Merlin gives up!

Many a small thing has been made large by using the right words.

But Merlin was a magician who believed in his own magic. And no magician can do well who believes such silly things as that!

So, for two days, Merlin pawed the air and muttered— and nothing happened.

How goes it, partner?

Behold! I am even now at my final touch of magic. Peace until I finish.

I think you'd better go home and practice on the weather, friend!

My helpers arrived. With Merlin out of the way, we went right to work patching up the old well. We even put in a pump so there would be a real fountain. Of course, all this was done in secret. Nobody else was allowed near the place.

We even set up fireworks on the roof of the chapel to add to the big event.

News of the dry fountain had traveled far and wide. A steady flow of people poured into the valley to see if my magic would work.

The night that all was ready, I sent word that the water had started again and that everybody could come and see. We set off the fireworks and the magic went off with a big bang.

It was a great night! I could hardly sleep when I finally got to bed.

After all this I decided to dress up as a poor man and wander alone through the country. Sandy wanted to stay behind for a little rest.

But I learned something new before I even left the valley. When I climbed up to visit some of the caves, one of them caught my eye right away.

Hello, Central!

The telephone crew had put in an office and phone the night before. News had just come through that King Arthur had heard of the magic and was on his way to see it.

I told the king of my plan to dress up as a poor man. He decided to go with me.

But more surprises were in store.

Get your *Camelot Weekly* here! All for two cents!

Something greater than kings had arrived: the newspaper and the newsboy! And I had started it!

I sat still, drunk with joy. Yes, this was heaven. I have tasted it this once, even though I may never taste it again!

HIGH TIMES
IN THE VALLEY OF
HOLINESS!
THE WATER WORKS
ARE CORKED!

Merlin works his arts and fails! But THE BOSS scores on his first try.

THE HOLY WELL
IS UNCORKED AMID
OUTBURST OF
FIRE, SMOKE,
AND THUNDER!

About bedtime I took the king to my room. There I cut his hair and helped him try on his new poor man's clothes.

Dressed alike, we could pass for small farmers. The problem was that we must not only look like poor people, but act like them as well.

Look humble, Sire— and quickly!

Sorry! I was planning a war in my head and didn't see him!

If only I had known what it would be like! If anybody wants to make his living passing off a king for a poor man, let him! I learned my lesson the hard way!

I spent a day teaching the king how to act like a farmer.

Stoop those shoulders! Think *"My children are hungry."* Now, pretend you meet a farmer at his hut. What would you say to him?

You there! Bring me a seat!

It would be better if you called him *friend* or *brother*.

Brother? To a person like that?

But we are pretending to be people like that too!

How wonderful is truth!

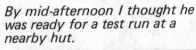

By mid-afternoon I thought he was ready for a test run at a nearby hut.

Have mercy! Everything has already been stolen!

Let me help you!

Leave at once, Sire! This woman is dying of the sickness that killed so many at Camelot two years ago!

Ye mean well and speak wisely. But I shall remain and help!

My daughter . . .

Here was a real hero! A king in commoner's clothes carried death in his arms so that a poor mother might take a last look at her child before she died.

By midnight it was all over, and we walked off into the darkness. All of a sudden I bumped into something.

We must cut them down!

There is no sense in that. It is too late for them to thank you, and the weather is bad.

Indeed, the next turn in the road was no better than the last! We kept on until we had put this place behind us. After all, we were strangers here, and it would be hard to tell people I was traveling with their king.

We came to another hut.

Sell us your house and go! We are poor company, having just left those that died of the spotted death!*

It was good of the king, but not necessary. Everyone in the area had suffered from the sickness he spoke of. They could not catch it again. So when this woman learned that we were lost travelers, she made us very welcome.

We slept. Later we learned from our hosts the tale of what we had seen the night before. The local noble had been killed and his house burned.

He was a man known for his evil ways. But there was no trial. A poor family that had been treated badly by him was blamed for his death. Eighteen people were hanged to pay for the life of one cruel noble.

*smallpox, a fearful disease

Leaving the king behind, I walked to town the next morning with the husband. We spoke very openly with each other.

The devil's work has been done on good people. The cruel old noble only got what he deserved!

Even though you may be a spy, and your words a trap for a poor farmer, they sound good to my ears. I would gladly be hanged just to have heard that!

You see, a man is a man at bottom. Whole ages of evil deeds can't crush that.

Still, as we walked along, I was surprised by this man's speech to a stranger.

Toward the monk he showed great respect.

To the gentleman he was meek and humble.

But when a slave passed by, his nose was in the air.

There are times when one would like to hang the whole human race and finish the joke.

I met Dowley, the rich village blacksmith. Marco, the farmer, was proud to have him as a friend. We got along well at once, as I had many such self-made men under me at the factory back in Connecticut.

I invited Dowley and other friends to dine with us on Sunday. Marco looked very troubled.

You must allow me to have these people come for lunch. I'll pay the costs. You and your wife have been very good to us.

'Tis nothing—we have very little to offer!

The best a man has, freely given, is always something. A prince can do no more!

I sent Marco to invite more friends. Then I set about ordering things for a feast. I bought dishes, tables, chairs, food. I never care to do things in a quiet way. It's got to be showy or I don't want any part of it.

It was near sunset when the things began to arrive. It was all I could do to keep the Marco family from fainting.

Sunday was one of those rich fall days when it is heaven to be outdoors. Dowley was in fine spirits, and I soon had him telling us his story.

Starting out as an orphan, he worked hard. Soon he was rich.

On my table there is fresh meat two times every month and white bread every Sunday!

But if a fellow has a good heart, I don't care how poor he is, I say we are equals. And here's my hand to prove it!

The king took Dowley's hand as gladly as a lady would take a fish. But it was good because Dowley thought he felt unworthy to shake this rich man's hand.

The food that day was like nothing this crowd had ever seen before!

Well, I think our meal is ready! Come, eat well!

Yes, the air had been let out of Dowley. He looked a little like a balloon that's been stepped on by a cow.

After dinner Arthur took a nap. The rest of us talked of business and money.

In your country, brother, what is the wage for a farmer?

Two cents a day!

Ha! With us it's double that! For a toolmaker we pay ten cents. How about you?

We pay only five cents for a toolmaker. But what do you pay for a pound of salt?

Twenty cents!

Well, we pay only five. You see, your wages are only higher in name, not in fact.

Hear him! Our wages are double. You've said so yourself!

But the important thing is how much you can buy with your wages!

It was hopeless. What these people wanted was high wages. They didn't seem to care whether their money could buy anything or not. The king joined us just as our talk really began to heat up.

Some say the onion is but a berry. Others say that plums and apples should be picked green!

This farmer is out of his mind!

One would take away our high wages! The other is crazy! Kill them, I say! Kill them both!

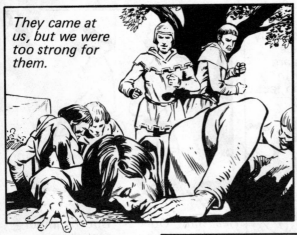

They came at us, but we were too strong for them.

I told the king to get out of there as fast as he could.

In minutes there was a mob on our trail!

Things looked quite bad until . . .

Stop! Or ye be dead men!

But sir, these be madmen!

We are peaceful strangers who but for your help would have been killed by this mob!

Bring horses for these people!

For a time it seemed we were saved.

What meaneth this joke?

Put up the slaves and sell them!

Yes, we were sold like pigs. We were sold to a slave dealer. It only shows that there is no difference between a king and a tramp if you don't know which is the king.

So the king fell from the highest place to the lowest. But I think the thing that really burned him most was the low price he went for. He was sold for seven dollars. I was sold for nine.

We had a rough time of it for a month. Finally, on the question of owning slaves, the king was all for having it stopped. He had not cared a bit before.

Now I was more than ready to set us free. When I saw some telephone wires, I began to think of a plan.

That night I picked the lock to my cell and set off to get things moving.

Clarence, the king is here and in danger. Send 500 knights with Lancelot! And do it quickly!

But when I returned to the slave area . . .

Seems one of the slaves got away! When the master started beating the others, they turned on him and killed him.

And now?

By Roman law, if one slave killeth his master, all slaves of that man must die!

Things were very bad.

And then things got worse!

He's a slave, too!

Stop! I am Arthur, king of Britain!

All hail!

The knights arrived just in time...

On your knees to the king, you rascals. He who fails will die!

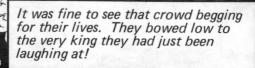

It was fine to see that crowd begging for their lives. They bowed low to the very king they had just been laughing at!

Home again in Camelot, I discovered this item in the morning paper.

Know all, that the great lord Sir Sagramor has lowered himself and agreed to meet The Boss in combat. Time set is 10 o'clock in the morning on the 16th. day of the month.

From that day there was talk of nothing else in all of Britain. Everyone knew that this was a fight between Merlin and myself. It was to be a battle for power between the two greatest magicians in the world.

It was well known that Merlin had been busy for days putting a spell* on Sir Sagramor's armor. He hoped his magic would keep Sir Sagramor safe from any blows I might strike. When the great day came, not a single seat was left on the field.

Sir Sagramor rode out first, a tower of iron. I rode out wearing a simple pair of tights. Armor was too much for me.

*a kind of magic in which words are used to harm or protect something

When the signal was given, Sir Sagramor rode at me with fire in his eyes. But I sat still swinging the loop of my lasso. Suddenly I tossed the rope toward him.

The rope pulled tight and yanked Sir Sagramor out of his saddle. The crowd went clear out of their seats with joy! They'd never seen a cowboy act before.

At first many knights wanted to fight me. But after I roped five others down, they began to change their minds. At that moment, in rode Sir Lancelot like a blast of winter wind.

But Sir Lancelot, the knight no one had been able to beat, went down too. Now that I had won, it was time to show the people what else I could do for them.

I no longer felt I had to work in secret. So the very next day I showed them my hidden schools and factories.

Soon there were no more slaves. Phonographs, sewing machines, and other modern wonders were everywhere. We even had railroads! I put the knights to work, too, although they would not give up their armor.

Yes, things were moving along. In a few years we had a steamboat on the Thames River. I was getting ready to send a ship or two to discover America.

Sandy took her place again at my side. This time we were married. A grand wedding was given to us by the king.

Things went along well. Soon we had a beautiful daughter. Sandy named her Hello Central after the telephone lines which had saved my life and King Arthur's as well.

But one day Sandy came to me looking troubled.

Speak, dear! What is it?

Hello Central is ill!

Our little darling had lived in my arms much of her small life. Often I could calm her and get her to laugh when even her mother couldn't.

But some strange sickness had struck our child. The doctors thought we should take her on a sea voyage for her health.

While I was away on the voyage, something took place in the kingdom that changed all my grand plans. King Arthur, whose heart could not think evil of a friend, learned of Sir Lancelot's love for Queen Guenivere.

Because of Sir Lancelot's love for the queen, the kingdom was split in two. There was a terrible battle. The king was killed. The Church took over the land and changed all my beautiful plans.

I left Sandy and the child, who was much better, in a warmer land. I returned to England and found that everything was back in the dark ages, the way it had been when I first arrived there.

The Church closed all my schools and factories. I came back to find the country in a very troubled state.

The Church is master now, and they have all the knights that are left on their side!

There is nothing to do but fight it out.

And so Clarence and I, with a handful of our youngest students, came to stand against an army of 30,000 knights.

Now speak, and it will be as you decide. Shall we stay out of battle and leave the field?

No! No!

The final attack came in waves. When the first line of knights ran into our mine field,* it blew up, leaving a huge hole. When the second group moved in, we filled the hole with water and turned on the electric fence.

This way we electro-cuted** or drowned the other army without the loss of even one of our boys.

But how dangerous is fortune! I will let the record end here.

*a field in which hidden bombs are planted
**killed someone by giving him a great electric shock

Merlin was quite pleased with himself. In his joy he reached out and grabbed the end of one of our 'hot' wires! In a second he was dead with a frozen smile on his face.

The Boss *never moved.* He sleeps like a stone. We have put his body in a place where it will never be found. We leave this paper with our Boss!

The dawn had almost come when I laid the papers aside and went to the stranger's room.

I peeped in and there he lay, moving about as sick people do in a fever.

" . . . to the king . . . the drawbridge . . . man the battlements . . . turn out the . . .

The Boss was getting together his last plans. But he never finished them!

THE END

words to know

King Arthur's court	magician	pilgrims
joust	tournaments	spell
eclipse	the Holy Grail	electrocuted
dungeon	conscience	

questions

1. How did the Connecticut Yankee get to Camelot?

2. How did Mark Twain happen to hear the story that he tells in this book?

3. Name some of the "miracles" that the Connecticut Yankee performed at Camelot. Would we in the twentieth century have reacted differently to them than the people of King Arthur's time? Explain.

4. What were some of the improvements made by the Connecticut Yankee? Do you think they helped the people of England?

5. Who usually decided whether a person would live or die? Do you like the idea? Why or why not?

6. The story of the Connecticut Yankee is funny in many places. But there are also examples of foolishness and cruelty. Name some of them, and tell how you feel about them.

7. What does the Connecticut Yankee mean when he says (on page 49) that " . . . there is no difference between a king and a tramp if you don't know which is the king"?

8. How did the Connecticut Yankee get back into his own time, the nineteenth century?